Angelina Balle___a's

How to be a Ballet Star

Story by Katharine Holabird Illustrations by Helen Craig

Do you *love* dancing and want to be a little ballerina?
You'll need to practise your steps all of the time.

But arabesques can cause
problems in the kitchen!

Little ballerinas should never stay
up too late practising.

Or they might be very sorry
the next day.

Even little ballerinas can feel
sad and lonely sometimes.

But doing cartwheels with a best friend
makes everyone happy again.

Little ballerinas don't always
get the lead role,

but they are truly brave and do their best
whatever part they are given.

Sometimes
little ballerinas get
teased . . .

but they soon
show everyone how fast
and fearless they are.

Little ballerinas can
be impatient . . .

and even
cross sometimes.

But they can be very kind and
understanding with little mouselings too.

Little ballerinas always love to dance,
but they like lots of other things as well.

Little ballerinas can
sometimes feel jealous.

Dancing makes everything
all right again.

Little ballerinas adore dressing up
in different costumes.

It's the best fun ever!

After a hard day's dancing,

every little ballerina
needs a cuddle.

Little ballerinas love their ballet teachers,

and are always ready to help.

Little ballerinas sometimes
make mistakes onstage.

In their dreams they'll be perfect.

Happy dancing!

Angelina's Red Nose Day Dance

(to the tune of 'If You're Happy and You Know It')

Why don't you get sponsored to do the Red Nose Day Dance with your friends or classmates?
For more information and to download a sponsorship form go to
www.rednoseday.com

If you're a ballerina, point your toes.
If you're a ballerina, point your toes.
If you're a ballerina, just like little Angelina,
It's fun to point your toes and wiggle your nose.

If you're a ballerina, raise your arms.
If you're a ballerina, raise your arms.
If you're a ballerina, just like little Angelina,
It's fun to raise your arms and wiggle your nose.

If you're a ballerina, twirl around.
If you're a ballerina, twirl around.
If you're a ballerina, just like little Angelina,
It's fun to twirl around and wiggle your nose.

If you're a ballerina, jump up high.
If you're a ballerina, jump up high.
If you're a ballerina, just like little Angelina,
It's fun to jump up high and wiggle your nose.

If you're a ballerina, take a bow.
If you're a ballerina, take a bow.
If you're a ballerina, just like little Angelina,
It's fun to take a bow and wiggle your nose.

All About Comic Relief

Comic Relief was launched in 1985 in response to the
devastating famine in Ethiopia and Sudan.

Since then, a total of nine Red Nose Days have raised more than
£280 million, with that money being used to help change the lives
of many thousands of people here in the UK as well as in Africa.
People like eleven-year-old Gethyn from Wales, who has had to care
for his sick mum and dad, and seventy-two-year-old Jean from Kenya,
who's been able to move into decent housing for the first time in her life.

Comic Relief's success is a tribute to the enduring
generosity of the general public. Because you have bought and
read this book, Comic Relief will be able to help even more
people change their lives for the better – thank you
and enjoy the Angelina Red Nose Day Dance!

Angelina is absolutely thrilled to be helping Comic Relief, and so are we. We hope you'll enjoy this special book and have fun twirling with Angelina in her Red Nose Day Dance.

With best wishes

Helen Craig

Katharine Holabird

PUFFIN BOOKS

Published by the Penguin Group
Penguin Books Ltd, 80 Strand, London WC2R 0RL, England
Penguin Group (USA), Inc., 375 Hudson Street, New York, New York 10014, USA
Penguin Books Australia Ltd, 250 Camberwell Road, Camberwell, Victoria 3124, Australia
Penguin Books Canada Ltd, 10 Alcorn Avenue, Toronto, Ontario, Canada M4V 3B2
Penguin Books India (P) Ltd, 11 Community Centre, Panchsheel Park, New Delhi –
110 017, India
Penguin Group (NZ), cnr Airborne and Rosedale Roads, Albany, Auckland 1310, New Zealand
Penguin Books (South Africa) (Pty) Ltd, 24 Sturdee Avenue, Rosebank 2196, South Africa

Penguin Books Ltd, Registered Offices: 80 Strand, London WC2R 0RL, England

www.penguin.com

First published 2005
1 3 5 7 9 10 8 6 4 2

Made and printed in Italy by Printer Trento Srl

British Library Cataloguing in Publication Data
A CIP catalogue record for this book is available from the British Library

ISBN 0-141-50019-0

To find out more about Angelina, visit her website at www.angelinaballerina.com

The publishers would like to thank Printer Trento for their contribution to this book.
Printed on GardaMatt Art, kindly supplied by Cartiere del Garda spa